KV-677-381

A MONSTER CALLED
CHARLIE

Also by Margrit Cruickshank
in Children's Poolbeg

S.K.U.N.K. and the Ozone Conspiracy
S.K.U.N.K. and the Nuclear Waste Plot
S.K.U.N.K. and the Splitting Earth

and for teenagers
Circling the Triangle

This book belongs to

_____

Children's
POOLBEG

ABOUT THE AUTHOR

Margrit Cruickshank was born in Scotland. She moved to Ireland over twenty years ago and lives in Dublin with her family and her cats. Her works for children and teenagers have been greatly praised and she was shortlisted both for the Irish Books Award and for the Irish Children's Book Trust Bisto Book of the Year Award.

A MONSTER CALLED
CHARLIE

BY MARGRIT CRUICKSHANK
ILLUSTRATED BY ALISON KENNEDY QUILLINAN

First published 1992 by
Poolbeg Press Ltd
Knocksedan House,
Swords, Co Dublin, Ireland

© Margrit Cruickshank, 1992

The moral right of the author has been asserted.

Poolbeg Press receives assistance from
The Arts Council/An Chomhairle Ealaíon, Ireland.

ISBN 1 85371 201 9

A catalogue record for this book is available from the British Library.

All rights reserved. No part of this publication may be reproduced or transmitted in any form
or by any means, electronic or mechanical, including photography, recording, or any information
storage or retrieval system, without permission in writing from the publisher. The book is sold
subject to the condition that it shall not, by way of trade or otherwise, be lent, resold or otherwise
circulated without the publisher's prior consent in any form of binding or cover other than that
in which it is published and without a similar condition including this condition being imposed
on the subsequent purchaser.

Cover design by Alison Kennedy Quillinan
Set by Richard Parfrey in ITC Stone Serif 12/17
Printed by The Guernsey Press Company Ltd,
Vale, Guernsey, Channel Islands

For Janetta

Contents

1

In Which Charlie Meets Daniel

It was Saturday morning and Daniel was alone in the house.

His parents were at the supermarket, his sister Kate had gone swimming and his grandmother, who was minding him, had fallen asleep in the garden.

So when the doorbell rang, he had a problem. He knew he wasn't allowed to open the door by himself but he didn't want to wake his grandmother. He hesitated.

The doorbell rang again.

Daniel made up his mind. He dragged a stool out into the hall, climbed up on it, turned back the latch and opened the front door.

And there on the mat stood a monster.

It wasn't a big monster. It wasn't a huge scaly

monster that breathed fire at you. Or a big hairy monster that could crush you with one paw tied behind its back. In fact, it was really quite small. It had a fat, furry, green tummy, a small snouty head, big black eyes with long blue eyelashes, two stumpy scaly wings and a short fat scaly tail.

"Boo!" it said.

Daniel stared.

"Well? Aren't you going to run away?" it asked.

Daniel looked down at it. Its eyes were crossed and the whiskers on its head were waving up and down and making a strange screeching sound, like a radio that isn't tuned to the right station. It didn't look scary at all.

"I am Saint Patrick," it said. "I am a great big hairy dragon and I have come to eat you all up."

"You're who?" Daniel asked.

"I am Saint Patrick? A great big hairy dragon?" The monster sounded less certain.

"Saint Patrick was a saint," Daniel pointed out. "He banished all the snakes from Ireland. Mrs Murphy told us about him in school."

"Oh." The monster thought for a minute.

Then it crossed its eyes and waved its whiskers up and down again. "Fo, fe, fi, fum!" it shouted loudly. "I smell the blood of an English Mum!"

Daniel started to giggle. "It's fe, fi, fo, fum," he said. "And my Mum's Irish."

"Oh," the monster said again. "Are you sure about Saint Patrick?" it asked. "I mean, I read about him in a book about Earth."

"Of course I'm sure," Daniel answered. "Everyone knows about Saint Patrick." Then he realised what the monster had just said. "You read about him in a book about *where*?" he asked.

"About Earth. That is where we are, isn't it?"

Daniel gulped. "Where…where do you come from, then?"

"Charliopeaia Minor."

"Where?"

"Charliopeaia Minor," the monster repeated impatiently. "Are you thick?"

Daniel tried to imagine the map of the sky which Kate had stuck on her bedroom wall. There were an awful lot of stars and planets on it. Could there be one called—whatever the monster had said? "Where's that?" he asked.

The monster waved a paw into the sky behind its shoulder. "Out there," it said vaguely.

Daniel looked up, half-expecting to see a new planet behind Mrs Fitzgerald's television aerial or a spaceship hovering over the street. Everything was normal.

"How did you get here?" he asked.

Two tears welled out of the monster's black eyes and trickled down its cheeks to soak into the fur of its tummy. "The spaceship wasn't working properly," it said, "and they didn't know if we'd manage to get home or not. So they decided to throw out everything they didn't need to make it lighter. And when there was nothing left to throw out, they threw out *me*."

"Oh you poor thing," Daniel said. "How could they?"

"They just opened the door and pushed."

The monster looked so sad, standing there with tears rolling down its face, that Daniel moved his stool out of the way and opened the door wider.

"Why don't you come in?" he said.

2

In Which Charlie Finds a Name and a Home

The monster cleaned its webbed feet carefully on the mat and waddled through to the kitchen. It looked round, as if searching for something, saw the pot-stand, went over to it, took out two of the biggest saucepans and placed them in the middle of the kitchen floor. It squeezed itself into one of them and sat there, looking at Daniel expectantly.

Daniel tried not to laugh.

"Well?" the monster asked.

"Sorry?"

The monster's whiskers started to hum softly. "If we were in Charliopeaia Minor and you were me," it said, "I'd have asked me a long time ago if I wanted anything to eat."

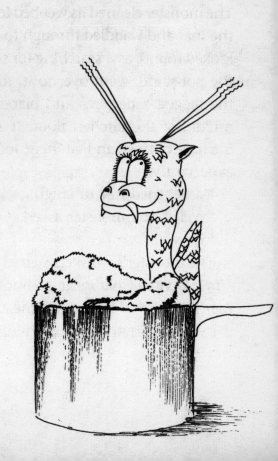

"Do you?" Daniel asked. He wondered what monsters from Charli-whatever-it-was ate. He hoped it was something simple like bread and jam.

"Mmmm," the monster said, drooling. "Seeing as how you asked, I'd like a grunch-and-whoppit sandwich. With loads of lummy-lushus sauce.

"Please," it added.

Daniel thought quickly. "We don't have that," he said, "but I can give you something just as nice."

"Are you sure it's just as nice?"

"Yes." Daniel tried to sound as if he was.

He made a jam sandwich as quickly as he could and handed it to the monster. It waited politely while he made one for himself.

"Aren't you going to sit down?" it asked, waving the sandwich towards the second saucepan and dripping raspberry jam on the kitchen floor.

"Er...we usually sit at the table," Daniel explained.

"Oh." The monster looked embarrassed. Then

it squeezed slowly out of the saucepan, waddled over to the kitchen table, looked up at it, sighed, put the sandwich in its mouth and clambered up the nearest stool. From there, it scrambled onto the table. It sat down, chewed a couple of times, swallowed and looked at him expectantly again. "That was nice," it said. "Are there any more?"

"We usually sit *at* the table, not *on* it," Daniel said, spreading another slice of bread. "We sit on a stool." He got onto a stool and patted the one next to him. "Like this."

"Like this?" the monster said, clambering down onto the other stool.

"Yes."

"Strange," the monster muttered to itself.

For the next few minutes, they both concentrated on eating.

Then the monster wiped its mouth with a bright green claw, moving a smear of jam up to near its left ear. "Thank you..." It hesitated. "Oh dear," it said, "What would my mother think of me? I don't even know your name."

"That's okay," said Daniel. "My name's Daniel. What's yours?"

The monster hung its head. "I'm…" it started, in a very soft voice.

"Yes?" said Daniel encouragingly.

"I'm Hey-you-what's-its-name," the monster whispered, very quickly.

"You're what?"

"Hey…you…what's…its…name. My mother always seems to be in a rush and she keeps forgetting who I am." It sniffed and rubbed its eyes, moving the smear of raspberry jam back down to its mouth again.

"Don't you have any other name?"

"I don't know." The monster sniffed some more.

"I'll call you Charlie, then," Daniel decided. "After the planet you come from."

"Charlie?" The monster tried it out. It smiled. "Charlie!" it said again. It thought for a moment. "Charliopeaia Minor would sound nicer," it suggested.

"Charlie," Daniel said firmly.

"Oh. Is that an Earth name?"

"Yes. Lots of boys on Earth are called Charlie."

"Lots of boys," the monster repeated, seeming to shrink down on the stool. It hung its head and tears oozed out between its bright blue eyelashes.

Daniel looked at it more closely. "You *are* a boy, aren't you?" he asked.

The monster raised its head and wiped its eyes again. "Do I look like one?" it asked. It sounded hurt.

"Of course you don't," Daniel said quickly. "Did I say boys? I meant boys and girls. Charlie can be both. It's a sort of very special name." He crossed his fingers and hoped the monster would believe him.

"A very special name," the monster said, a smile breaking out on her peagreen face. "If it's very special, that's fine."

She licked a front claw and combed her whiskers. "Charlie," she said thoughtfully. "Charlie. Thank you, Daniel; it's nice." To his surprise, she started to hum a little tune:

I once was a monster called Hey-you
But now I am Charlie. So say you
Don't remember my name,
Then you'll be to blame,
For Charlie is *special*. Okay, you?

I was lost and afraid and alone
(From a spaceship to Earth I'd been thrown)
But here on the ground
Just look what I've found:
I've a name and a friend and a home!

"You *will* be my friend and you *will* give me a home, won't you?" she asked.

Daniel had the feeling that things were going a bit too fast. "I'd love to be your friend and it would be great if you could come to live with us," he said anxiously, "but we'll have to ask Mummy and Daddy first."

"Oh." The monster's face fell. "Can't I stay here without meeting them? Grown-ups don't seem to like me much."

"Mummy and Daddy will." Daniel touched the wooden table. He remembered the time he'd tried to keep a stray kitten hidden in his bedroom and how angry his parents had been when they'd found out. His room hadn't been that smelly, either.

"Are they dangerous?" Charlie asked, her whiskers beginning to hum.

"Who? Kittens?"

"Your parents."

"No. Not really. I mean, when Mummy caught me and Kate racing snails in the front room last week, she shouted a lot. But she's not dangerous."

"I don't mind if they are," Charlie said loudly. She clambered down off the stool. She crossed her eyes and the humming from her whiskers grew louder. "I am a fierce Saint Patrick...er...I mean dragon," she squealed, "and if they don't let me stay I'll...I'll..."

"Shh! You'll wake Gran. And that's not the way to get round them."

Charlie uncrossed her eyes. "What is then?"

"You'll have to be very sweet and very harmless and make them feel very sorry for you."

"Like this?" the monster asked, turning her

webbed toes inwards, hanging her head and blinking her long blue eyelashes.

"That's it, Charlie," Daniel said. "That's just right."

But when Mr and Mrs Wilson got back from the shops, they didn't seem too pleased at the thought of a monster coming to stay.

"Absolutely not," said Mr Wilson. "You and Kate give us enough trouble as it is. If you want to bring something new into the house, why not make it a new cooker for your mother or a sports car for me?"

"Or the other way around," Mrs Wilson said sweetly. "I'm sure your father would love a new cooker."

"It's not funny!" Daniel yelled. "Can't you see Charlie's miserable? She told you: nobody loves her and they threw her out of her spaceship and she's got nowhere to go."

Mrs Wilson smiled at Charlie, who was standing in the middle of the floor, looking as lost and lonely and harmless and friendly and nice as she possibly could. "We wouldn't just put her out

into the street, Daniel. But the ISPCA knows how to look after strange animals. We can send her there."

"They'll put her in a cage and lock her up!" Daniel was horrified.

Charlie backed against the fridge, her eyes rolling, her whiskers squeaking in terror.

Daniel picked her up and hugged her. "Please, Mummy," he implored over the little monster's head. "Look how frightened she is. She trusts me. Please!"

Mrs Wilson looked at Mr Wilson. He shrugged. "Okay, Daniel. We'll let her stay. But only until her people come back for her."

"They do know where you are, don't they...er...Charlie?" Mrs Wilson asked.

Charlie squirmed and looked down at the claws on her green webbed feet.

"Of course they do," Daniel said. "As soon as they get back home, they'll send a spaceship to collect her. Won't they, Charlie?" He gave Charlie a dig.

"Er...Yes," Charlie said miserably.

"A spaceship?" Mrs Wilson frowned. "Well, I

suppose so. As long as it doesn't land on my lawn and ruin it." She grinned. "It'll be fun to see what the neighbours say."

"They'll come at night and beam Charlie up," Daniel said quickly. "Like they do on the telly. They won't harm the lawn at all and nobody will see anything."

"Is that right?" Mrs Wilson asked Charlie.

The little monster looked up at Daniel. He frowned back at her.

"Er...yes," she said again, even more miserably.

And that's how Charlie got to stay.

3

In Which Charlie Learns to Play Football and Gives a Flying Lesson

After lunch, Daniel took Charlie into the garden. His sister Kate came too.

"Let's play football," she suggested. She stuck two sticks into the lawn. "They'll be the goalposts. Do you want to be goalkeeper first, Charlie?"

"Yes, please," said Charlie excitedly.

Daniel took the ball to the other end of the lawn. He tried to dribble it past Kate. She stopped him. He tried again. On the third try, he got past her and shot at the goal.

Charlie watched the ball fly through the gap between the sticks.

"One goal to me!" Daniel shouted.

Charlie clapped her claws together. "Well done, Daniel!"

"Why weren't you in goal, you stupid monster?" yelled Kate. "I thought you were supposed to be goalie."

"I am," said Charlie happily.

Kate sighed. "Don't you know what a goalkeeper is supposed to do?"

"Do?" Charlie asked.

Daniel took her by the shoulders and pushed her into position between the two sticks. "Stay there," he said. "And try to keep the ball out. It's Kate's turn to shoot."

"Shoot?" Charlie's whiskers hummed in alarm. She squirmed out of Daniel's grasp and tried to hide behind his legs. "You didn't tell me you were going to use guns!"

"Shoot means kick the ball between the goalposts," Kate told her. "Nobody's trying to kill you, you twit."

"Oh," Charlie said.

"The goalkeeper has to stop the ball."

"You should have told me," Charlie muttered. "We don't have games like this on Charliopeaia Minor." She smiled a lopsided smile, smoothed her whiskers straight and waddled back to her

position between the two sticks. "Now that I know that's what a goalkeeper does, I'll certainly stop the ball for you."

She watched intently as Kate dribbled past Daniel, drew back her foot and kicked. The ball flew into the air.

There was a loud screeching noise, Charlie's eyes crossed, her whiskers waved about like windscreen wipers in a cloudburst. And the ball exploded.

"How did you do that, Charlie?" Daniel asked, looking in awe at the pieces of plastic scattered across the lawn. "Was it a death-ray? Can you blow up *anything*?"

To his surprise, instead of looking pleased with herself, Charlie slumped down onto the lawn and put her paws over her head. "I'm sorry," she whimpered. "I forgot. I know I'm not supposed to and I promise I won't do it again."

"Do what?" Daniel asked. "What exactly did you do?"

"I don't want to talk about it," Charlie said miserably. "I shouldn't have used it."

"You're dead right, you shouldn't," Kate told

her. "That was my ball. You've ruined it!"

Tears started to trickle out of Charlie's eyes.

Daniel put his arm round Charlie's heaving shoulders. He glared at his sister. "Now look what you've done!"

"What *I've* done?"

Daniel gave the little monster a hug. "I know, Charlie. Let's do something else. You choose what to do this time."

Charlie cheered up. "We could have a flying contest," she suggested. "We do that at home."

"A flying contest?" Daniel forgot about the death-ray. "Do you mean you can fly?"

"Of course I can." Charlie drew herself up proudly. "All Charliopeaians can fly. Can't you?"

"Well, yes. In an aeroplane."

"Let's see you flying, Charlie," Kate urged. "Fly up on to the roof. I dare you!"

Charlie looked up at the roof of the Wilsons' house. It was very high. She hopped from one webbed foot to the other. "Er…Maybe we should wait until tomorrow. I mean, you two will need time to practise."

"You're scared," Kate said.

Daniel kicked his sister. "Don't mind her, Charlie. I know you're not scared."

"You do?" It came out half-way between a question and a statement.

"She is so scared," Kate said. "She's a hopeless goalie and I bet she can't fly either. All she can do is wreck footballs."

"I can fly." Charlie looked round the garden. She waddled over to the rockery and scrambled up it until she was standing on the topmost stone. She flapped her tiny scaly wings and started to sing:

In Charliopeaia where the breeze
Glides over thunkelberry trees,
O'er glades where frumpus bushes grow
We love to flutter to and fro;
We loop the loop, we dive down low
We fly where no man dares to go.
We're just like *turkeys* in the air!
All Charliopeaians fly! So there!

She took a deep breath, crossed her eyes, and waggled her whiskers. Then she flapped her

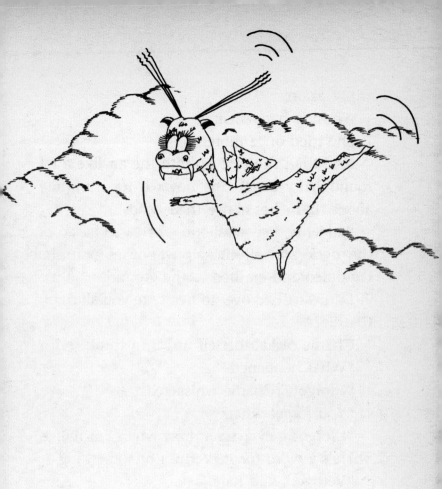

wings again.

Nothing happened.

She tried once more.

And then she rose up into the air like a fat round hairy angel. She hovered for a minute about six inches above their heads.

Suddenly, like a balloon when you let go of the neck and all the air whooshes out, she crumpled and crashed to the ground.

Daniel rushed over to her. "Are you all right, Charlie?"

Charlie picked herself up. "I...I think so."

"What happened?"

"I forgot," Charlie whispered.

"You forgot what?"

"I forgot I always get dizzy when I'm flying. There's a word for it. Verruca or something."

"Vertigo," said Kate.

"Whatever. I've always had it. Since I was a baby. My mother never forgave me for it." Charlie's voice broke. "She said I was a disgrace to the whole family." And she threw herself, sobbing loudly, into Daniel's arms.

"Think of something!" Daniel hissed at his

sister.

"What?"

"I don't know. Just think of something to take her mind off flying!"

4

In Which Charlie Travels on a Bus

Kate suggested taking Charlie to the park, so Daniel got his mother's big round shopping basket out from under the stairs. Charlie jumped into it. "This is nice," she said. She sat up in the basket and wound her scaly little tail neatly round her green webbed toes. "Have you got one, too?"

"Got what?" Daniel asked, putting on his anorak.

"A basket, of course."

"What about a basket?"

"Have you and Kate got one? Or are you hoping to share mine? Because, if you are, it's going to be very crowded."

"We're going on the bus, Charlie."

Charlie looked worried. "If you're going on

the bus and I'm going in this basket, how will I know where to find you?"

Kate groaned. "You are going to hide in that basket so that nobody will see you, and Daniel and I are going to carry you to the bus stop and take you on the bus with us," she told her. "And if you don't duck down and let me put this towel over you, we'll miss the bus. Is that clear? Or do I have to spell it out to you?"

"You remind me of my mother," Charlie said in a very small voice.

Daniel pressed the little monster down into the bottom of the basket and covered her with a bath towel. "Just curl up, Charlie, and stay quiet. You'll be all right."

"Promise?"

"Cross my heart."

What neither Kate nor Daniel had realised was that McCavities, the biggest shop in town, was having an extra-special, unbelievable, amazing, stupendous, once-in-a-lifetime, give-away, closing-down sale that very day.

At each stop, more and more women boarded the bus, all headed for the centre of town. Soon every seat was taken and people were standing in the aisle.

"Ahem!"

Daniel looked up to find a red face glaring down at him. He looked away quickly.

"Well?" the red face demanded.

Daniel didn't answer.

"Aren't you two children going to stand up then?" the red-faced lady asked. "Where are your manners?"

"I'll get up, Daniel," Kate whispered. "You mind Charlie." She put the basket on Daniel's knees.

The red-faced woman sat down, taking up all the space the basket and Kate had taken up before. She prodded Daniel. "What about my friend, sonny? Up you get, now."

Daniel looked at Kate.

The basket twitched. "Stand up, Daniel," it hissed. "Where are your manners? Didn't your mother tell you to let older people sit down? Mine did."

"What's that you're saying?" the red-faced woman snapped. "Are you being cheeky, young man?"

"Er...No." Terrified in case Charlie said anything else, Daniel dumped the basket on the floor and jumped to his feet.

"It's only a couple more stops," Kate whispered to him. "Just hope that Charlie keeps quiet," she said, more loudly, to the basket on the floor.

Charlie must have heard. She lay motionless and didn't make a sound. Until, that is, they came to the university and a student who had also been sitting in the back seat struggled past them to get off. He tripped over the basket. It fell on its side. The bath towel slipped. And Charlie rolled out.

She found herself surrounded by legs and feet: fat legs, thin legs, long legs, short legs, feet in high-heeled shoes, feet in runners, feet in boots and feet in heavy walking shoes. One foot had already kicked her basket over. What would they do to her next?

She panicked and dived under the nearest seat. But not before one of the women had seen her.

"A rat!" she screamed.

It was an old bus. Its engine was noisy and it rattled like a sackful of metal cans being shaken against a piece of corrugated iron. But even so, every passenger heard the scream.

In a flash, all the women had climbed onto the seats of the bus.

Above their shrieks, Daniel heard another sound. The screeching of Charlie's whiskers!

He remembered how easily Charlie had destroyed Kate's football. He had to find her—before she used whatever power she had on the people in the bus!

Getting down on his hands and knees, he searched under the seats. "Come on, Charlie! Come out, wherever you are!"

Two crossed eyes peered at him from the darkness. "They'll hurt me," Charlie moaned.

"No they won't. I promise. Get back into the basket quickly and we'll get you off the bus."

"Are you sure you promise?"

Kate was kneeling in the aisle too. "Come on, you idiot. Hurry up. Or they *will* get you."

The bus lurched as the driver pulled in to the kerb. The horde of hysterical passengers piled

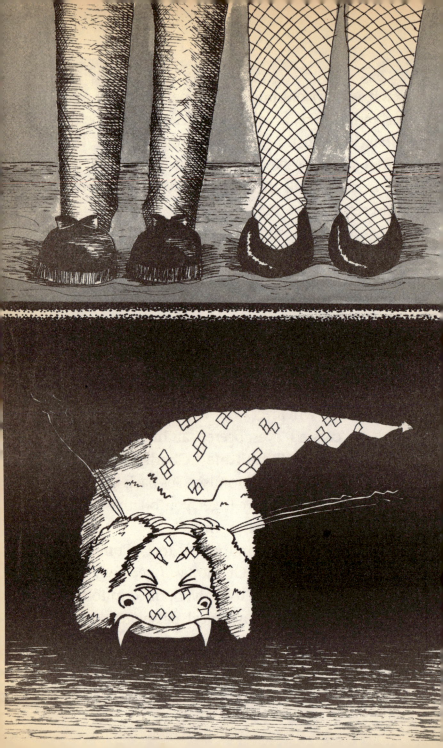

off. The driver took a huge spanner out of his tool kit.

"Come on, Charlie! Quickly. Or it'll be too late."

Charlie crawled out from under the seat. Her whiskers were bent, her fur was dusty, her eyes were still crossed.

"Get her into the basket!" hissed Kate.

Daniel gave the little monster a quick cuddle, stuffed her in the basket and covered her up again.

The driver suddenly noticed them. "What are you two kids doing there?" he demanded. "There's a dangerous animal loose in this bus somewhere. You'd better get off before you get hurt."

"Thanks," Daniel mumbled, dragging the basket down the aisle.

Kate took the other handle. She smiled sweetly at the driver as they passed him.

"I hope you catch it," Daniel said politely.

Charlie, thankfully, had the sense to say nothing till they got off the bus.

5

In Which Charlie Goes to the Park

Daniel and Kate stood at the park gates and looked round. It was crowded. People were everywhere, walking their dogs, sitting on the benches or lying in the sun.

Charlie poked her head out from under the bath towel. "So that's what a park looks like," she said. "We have them at home. For growing thunkelberry trees."

"Get back down!" Kate hissed at her.

Charlie started to scramble out of the basket.

"Get back!" Kate shoved her head back under the towel.

It poked out again. "It's stuffy in here. I want some fresh air. And I need to run around a bit."

Daniel pushed her back down again. "Just hold on, Charlie. For another few minutes."

"Why?" The head poked out again. "Nobody else is stuck in a basket. Even the dogs get to run around. Why shouldn't I?"

Again Daniel pushed her head back down. "Remember the women in the bus, Charlie. People will freak if they see you." He looked at Kate in despair. "There's nowhere quiet for us to let her out," he said. "What are we going to do?"

"There's the lake," Kate suggested.

"Lake? Did you say lake?" Charlie's head appeared again. Her eyes were crossed and her whiskers waggled and started to hum. "I'm sorry. I promise I'll behave. Only please don't throw me in the lake!"

"We wouldn't, Charlie," said Daniel. "We love you."

"We might," said Kate as she pushed her back down again. "So stay down there."

Kate hired a rowing boat from the hut at the edge of the water. She rowed Daniel and the basket containing Charlie out into the middle of the lake. Only then did she let Daniel lift the bath towel.

Charlie, cowering at the bottom of the basket, looked up at him with large anxious eyes. "I was good, wasn't I?" she asked. "You won't let Kate throw me in?"

"She was only joking," Daniel said. "You can come out of the basket now. No one can see you here."

Charlie tumbled out into the bottom of the boat. She shook herself, turned round a couple of times to see if her tail were still okay, brushed her whiskers straight and sat up.

She looked accusingly at Kate. "If you were my guest on Charliopeaia Minor," she said, "I wouldn't treat you like that. Not even my mother would treat you like that. Not even my mother would treat *me* like that," she added, looking more and more sorry for herself. "And she could be very hurtful."

"We're sorry if we upset you, Charlie," Kate said. "But it was for your own good."

"That's what my mother always says too," the monster muttered.

"You're out now, Charlie. And we're going to an island; you'll like that." Daniel gave her a hug.

"A real island on a real lake?" Charlie cheered up. "Like it says in my book about Earth? With dragons and maidens in distress on it?"

"Er...No. Not exactly. But you'll like it anyway. I promise."

"Great!"

Kate took up the oars and started rowing again. Charlie leant over the side of the boat and trailed a green claw in the water. Her eyes sparkled with excitement, her whiskers quivered and she started to sing:

I love to go a-boating,
A-boating on the sea,
In search of fair young maidens
To be rescued just by me.
I'll boat the sixty oceans
From Cape Zing to Zappatrain,
And when it's time for supper
I'll come boating home again.

Suddenly her whiskers began to waggle and hum alarmingly.

"What is it, Charlie?" Daniel asked.

"Fish!" Charlie said. "I can see loads of beautiful, fat, amazing, golden fish!"

"Yes. There's quite a lot of them in the lake," Kate agreed. "They're carp. A kind of big goldfish."

Charlie licked her lips. "Can you eat them?" she asked.

"My teacher says people eat them in China, but we don't eat them here." Kate was proud of her knowledge.

"Oh," Charlie said. She stared back down into the water again.

Kate turned round to see how far she still had to row. Daniel looked too. And Charlie? Charlie clambered up onto the side of the boat, swayed for a split second, and then dived with a plump! into the lake.

Daniel and Kate heard the splash. They whirled round.

All they could see were rings expanding in the dark water.

They waited for Charlie to come up.

A few bubbles rose to the surface.

Daniel looked worriedly at Kate. "Do you

think she can swim?"

"I don't know," Kate said. She tried to smile reassuringly. "Most animals can swim. I'm sure she can too."

"She's supposed to be able to fly and you know how well she does that."

"I know." Kate frowned. "Do you think I should jump in and rescue her? They say you shouldn't."

"You can't just let her drown!"

More bubbles rose. But Kate still hesitated. "You're supposed to stay somewhere safe and throw something out to someone when they're in trouble in the water. We learnt that at swimming lessons. Otherwise both of you can drown."

Still more bubbles floated up.

"She's drowning now!" Daniel begged her. "Do something!"

And then, suddenly, spraying water in every direction like a garden sprinkler, Charlie's head appeared.

"Aargh!" she spluttered. "Help!! It's wet in here! Get me out!"

Kate had pulled off her jumper. She held on

to one sleeve and threw the rest of it towards Charlie. "Catch the end!" she shouted.

Charlie threshed the water with her webbed paws. She floated slowly backwards. She tried again.

The harder she tried to reach the jumper, the faster backwards she swam.

"Hold the jumper, Daniel. Don't let go of it— but don't let her pull you in, either." Kate passed her jumper over to Daniel and tried to row nearer to Charlie.

But the closer she came, the more the monster flapped with her hands and feet and the faster backwards she went.

6

In Which Charlie Meets the Police

Suddenly another boat appeared. "It's okay, you two," the man in the boat shouted across to them. "I'll get it!"

He grasped Charlie under her stumpy little wings and hoisted her into the boat. Charlie collapsed in a moaning wet heap.

The man stared down at her. He frowned. Then he rubbed his head, as if not quite believing what he'd seen, and looked over to Daniel and Kate in the other boat. "Is this yours?" he asked.

"No," said Kate.

"Yes," said Daniel. "Is she okay?"

The man studied the sodden, woebegone heap at the bottom of his boat. "It's alive, anyway. What on earth is it?"

"It's me. And I'm nothing on Earth. I'm a Charliopeaian. And I think I'm going to die," moaned the heap.

"Get up and shake yourself, you idiot," shouted Kate.

"Thanks," the man said, squeezing the water out of his jacket after Charlie had done as she suggested. "It's just as well I don't have my best clothes on."

"I'm sorry," Daniel said. "And thank you very much for pulling her out. I thought she was going to drown."

"So did I," Charlie moaned softly. Her fur streamed water, her whiskers hung limply down over her nose and her breath still came in great gulps.

"The sooner we get somewhere warm and dry, the better," the man said. "I don't know if things like this catch pneumonia, but I don't think we should risk it."

Charlie raised her head. "I'm not a thing," she squeaked. "I told you: I'm a Charliopeaian." Her whiskers snapped up straight and started to hum again, hiccupping every time Charlie gulped for air.

"Sorry," the man said with a grin. He turned back to Kate. "Can you follow me in?"

As they neared the shore, Daniel noticed that a large crowd had gathered: there was no way they'd get out of the park now without people asking all sorts of questions. And how were they going to get home? They could hardly risk going on the bus with Charlie dripping water through the holes in the basket and making a noise like a miniature foghorn with the hiccups. Why on earth hadn't they stayed playing football in the garden?

The man who had rescued Charlie waited for them at the boathouse. At first Daniel couldn't see Charlie. Then he noticed a wet stain on the man's jacket over a bulge which jumped up and down with a loud hiccupping noise every few seconds. He grinned.

"All right! Make way there! Everyone out of the way!"

To Daniel's surprise, the crowd drew back. The man led them through it to a police car which had appeared, as if by magic, at the park gates.

A policeman opened the back door and waited for them all to get in.

"Where do you live, then, kids?" the man asked.

Kate gave their address while Daniel looked round the car, trying to remember every detail of it to tell his friends. Not only had he got a monster of his own, but he was being taken home in a police car! They'd be green with jealousy! Almost as green as Charlie's tummy, he thought with a grin.

"Got that, Constable?"

"Yes, Chief Inspector."

The car moved off.

A Chief Inspector! Daniel couldn't believe his ears. You only heard of them on the television!

Charlie sulked. She sat on Daniel's lap, wrapped in the bath towel from the basket, and stared at the floor of the car, her whiskers still giving the occasional burp. "I don't like Earth lakes," she muttered to no one in particular. "Or parks. I nearly drowned, you know. And nobody cares."

Daniel gave her an absent-minded hug.

The Chief Inspector looked down at the little monster. "Don't worry, whatever you are. We'll have you home in a jiffy. Put on the siren, Johnny, please."

The driver switched on the car siren.

Charlie sat up with a jerk.

"Who's that?" she screeched. She scrambled down into the bottom of the car and put her paws over her head. She peered anxiously up at Daniel. "If it's my mother, you will tell her it wasn't my fault, won't you?" she whispered before she curled up again in a tiny, shivering, squeaking heap.

Daniel pulled her back up onto his knee. "It's only the car siren," he said, "not another monster."

"Oh. The car siren. Is that all?"

"Yes."

Charlie sat up. "I never really thought it was anything else," she said carefully. "I'm not stupid, you know."

"Of course you're not, Charlie," Daniel said.

Kate just snorted.

Ten minutes later, three figures crept quietly into the Wilsons' house.

Upstairs, in his bedroom, Daniel rubbed Charlie down with a dry towel. "There, now, Charlie. Are you all right?"

Charlie crawled into bed and pulled the covers up over her ears. "If I died of pneumonia neither of you would care," she mumbled mournfully. "You preferred that policeman to me. If I could run you around in a car with a siren like my Mummy, I would."

Daniel put an arm round the lump under the bedclothes. "We love you, Charlie. You know that. And we're very glad you came to stay with us."

"Are you?" the lump asked.

"Of course we are."

The lump was silent for a minute. Then: "What about Kate?"

Daniel prodded his sister.

"I suppose I am, too, Charlie." She sighed. "Only promise me, you'll stay at home in future. I don't think I could stand taking you anywhere ever again."

7

In Which Charlie Gets to Know a Gorilla

The next day was Sunday so Mr and Mrs Wilson decided they would all go to the zoo.

"As long as we don't have to take Charlie," Kate said.

Daniel said nothing but he wore his anorak all the way there. And he rushed through the gates ahead of the others as soon as they arrived.

Kate ran to catch up with him. "Hold on!" she shouted. "I'm supposed to look after you."

She noticed the front of his anorak twitch. "Oh no! I don't believe it! You've got Charlie in there!"

Daniel looked round carefully and pulled down the zip of his anorak.

Charlie's head popped out. "That's better!"

she said. She took a few deep breaths. "I don't know how you Earth people manage," she complained, "having to suffocate every time you go anywhere. You're really very backward, you know. At least, in Charliopeaia Minor, we've learnt how to travel and see where we're going, both at the same time."

"We do too," Daniel started. "It's only..." He stopped.

"I thought you were told to leave Charlie at home?" Kate said coldly.

Charlie looked worried. "Why?" she asked. "Is this zoo-thing dangerous?"

"No," said Daniel.

"Yes," said Kate firmly. "Very dangerous. You'll have to keep hidden all the time in case a great big dangerous animal sees you and decides to gobble you up."

"Oh," said Charlie in a very small voice. "Gobble me up? Like a dragon would gobble me up?"

"Yes," said Kate, even more firmly.

Daniel felt the little monster tremble in his arms. He glared at his sister. "Don't listen to Kate, Charlie. There aren't any dragons. And nobody's going to hurt you."

"Why do you want me to hide, then?" Charlie asked. "Are you ashamed of me? Sometimes I think my mother was. That's why she got rid of me by sending me to Earth." Tears gathered in her big black eyes.

Daniel gave her a hug. "Of course we're not ashamed of you. It's just..." He tried to think of an answer.

"He wants you to hide because anywhere we've gone with you, it's been a disaster," Kate explained for him.

Charlie drew in her head and pushed it under Daniel's arm, trying to burrow as far into him as she could. "Nobody loves me here either," she wailed in a muffled voice. "I want to go home!"

Daniel hugged her tightly. "We all love you, Charlie. And today's going to be fun. Don't listen to Kate."

"Huh," Kate snorted. "I warn you, Daniel. If there's any trouble at all, I'll disown you. You'll have to sort it all out by yourself."

"There won't be any trouble," Daniel said.

Which all goes to prove how wrong you can be.

Everything was fine until they came to the gorilla house. The open space in front of it was grassed and contained a huge wooden climbing frame. It was separated from the public by a moat and a high wall.

A big black gorilla was standing in front of the moat, looking up at its keeper.

The keeper turned to the people who had crowded round to watch. "It's Hubert's birthday today!" he announced.

Everybody cheered.

The keeper threw the cardboard box he was holding towards the gorilla. It caught it, like a cricketer fielding a catch, examined it with a puzzled frown, and then tore it open.

Inside was a chocolate cake.

The crowd all went "Aah!"

Charlie poked her head out of Daniel's jacket. "What's happening?" she asked.

She saw Hubert the gorilla and the birthday cake. Her whiskers started to hum with excitement.

"Is that a spludpuddery cake?" she asked, sniffing the air. Her eyes lit up, she licked her lips and she started to sing:

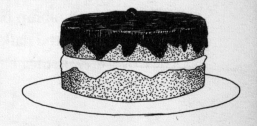

Spludpuddery cake, spludpuddery cake,
Oh how I love spludpuddery cake!
I'd eat it morning noon and night
I'd eat up every single bite!
Oh when I sleep and when I wake
I just *love* scrumptious spludpuddery cake!

"It's a chocolate cake," Kate said drily. "And it's Hubert's. So forget it."

"Is chocolate cake as good as spludpuddery cake?"

"Chocolate cake is brilliant!" Daniel said, his mouth watering.

"Then it must be like spludpuddery cake!"

Suddenly, before Daniel could stop her, Charlie had struggled out of his arms and scrambled onto the wall above the moat. She balanced unsteadily there for a minute, flapping her tiny scaly wings, and then flung herself off the wall towards the gorilla.

"Come back!" Daniel yelled.

Charlie's round plump body fell like a hairy rugby ball towards the dark water of the moat.

The crowd drew in their breath with a long hiss.

Then, just as it looked as if Charlie would plummet straight into the moat, she stopped falling and hung, hovering, just a few inches above the water, with a surprised expression on her face.

She took a deep breath, swung her tail round as if it were a rudder until she was facing the gorilla, and then swam forwards through the air towards the birthday cake.

The gorilla had its back turned and didn't see her coming.

Like a swallow catching flies in bad weather, Charlie swooped down round the gorilla's legs and made a grab for the cake.

Hubert realised what was happening and held on tight.

The cake split in two.

Hugging her piece tightly to her peagreen tummy, Charlie crashed to the ground.

For a moment Hubert just stared at her. Then he crammed his piece of cake into his mouth and started thumping his chest. He jumped up and down in front of Charlie, banging on his chest like a demented drummer while his teeth

chattered with the sound of a thousand casta-
nets. The crowd went mad.

"Come on, Hubert!" they shouted. "Get him,
boy!"

Daniel tried to scream but no sound came out
of his mouth. He shut his eyes tightly.

When he opened them again Charlie, still
clutching the piece of cake she'd stolen, was
waddling backwards towards the climbing frame.
Her eyes were crossed and her whiskers hummed
in terror.

The gorilla was still jumping up and down,
thumping and chattering.

The crowd was still cheering.

Daniel looked for the keeper, but he'd disap-
peared.

"Fly, Charlie! Get up into the air again!" he
shouted. "Quick! Before it's too late!"

The noise from the crowd drowned out his voice.

Suddenly, the gorilla stood still and stared at
the piece of cake in Charlie's claws.

Slowly, he moved forwards.

The noise from Charlie's whiskers grew even
louder.

The gorilla took another step forwards.

And then…

Kerpow!

The crowd went silent. Daniel turned his head and looked down into the enclosure.

Charlie was still backed up against the climbing frame, her whiskers were still humming like mad, the crowd was cheering again. But the gorilla was lying flat on its back with its paws in the air.

8

In Which Charlie Is Almost Shot

"Out of the way there! Get back!" Hubert's keeper pushed through the crowd. He was accompanied by another keeper, a woman, who had a rifle in her hands.

She raised the rifle and aimed it at Charlie.

"No!" Daniel threw himself at the lady keeper. "You can't shoot her! She's Charlie! She's our friend!"

"It's only a tranquilliser dart," the keeper said. "We'll just put her to sleep. Then we can examine her and find out what kind of creature she is."

"She's not a creature, she's Charlie! And she won't hurt anyone! She's very gentle and you mustn't shoot her and I can get her to come out, I know I can, only please don't shoot her!!!"

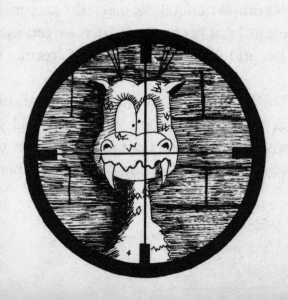

Daniel begged.

"It's who?" asked the first keeper.

"Charlie." Daniel felt for Kate's hand and held it tightly.

"And who in blue blazes is Charlie?"

"She's from outer space." Kate tried to make it sound normal and everyday. "And Daniel's right, she *is* quite harmless."

"Harmless? Did you see what she did to poor Hubert there?"

"It's only that she's frightened," Daniel pleaded. "Hubert was going to jump at her."

"*She's* frightened?" The red-haired keeper stared at Charlie, his mouth open. "She knocks a twenty-stone gorilla out cold and you tell me *she's* frightened!"

"She is." Kate backed Daniel up. "And it was only self-defence. She's an awful coward, really, and needs someone to look after her."

The lady keeper looked down at them with a smile. "You two, I suppose?"

"Well, yes."

"All right then, Superkids. Get her out of there. Before she harms Henrietta."

To Daniel's horror, another gorilla had come out of the gorilla house and was shambling over to Hubert's motionless body.

He leant over the barrier. "Come on, Charlie. Come back up. No one's going to hurt you."

Charlie looked from the second gorilla to the crowd. The gorilla was uneasy, making small worried chattering noises as she prodded her mate. The crowd was just as restless and much noisier. She backed further against the climbing frame.

"Come on, Charlie," Daniel shouted. "You're Saint Patrick the dragon, remember. Big and bad and fearless. Just fly back out and we'll take you home."

Charlie's ears drooped. "No," she muttered.

"Hurry up!" Daniel yelled.

"I'm scared," Charlie moaned. "You know I can't fly."

"You flew in," Daniel shouted. "If you can fly in, you can fly out."

"That was different."

Kate had been thinking. "You don't have a rope, do you?" she asked the lady keeper.

"There's one in the jeep. You get it, Dick, while I stay here with the gun. Just in case either of them needs it."

"Come over here, Charlie," Daniel pleaded. "Close to the moat. You don't want to be shot, do you?"

Charlie looked at the female gorilla again. Then she looked up at the wall. She scrambled up the first rung of the climbing frame. "I...I think I'll stay here, if it's all the same to you."

Kate groaned. "Don't be an idiot," she shouted. "The keeper's gone to get a rope. Come over to the moat so that we can throw it to you when he gets back."

Charlie hesitated. The female gorilla was now sitting beside her mate, her hand over her face, rocking backwards and forwards and groaning to herself. Charlie looked at the crowd.

She scrambled back down from the climbing frame and sidled up to the moat.

The crowd cheered. Someone threw a bag of crisps.

Charlie ignored it. She tried to look dignified but, with her tail still between her legs and her eyes still crossed, it was difficult.

Finally the red-haired keeper came back with a length of rope. He threw one end of it to Charlie.

"Can you tie it round you?" suggested Kate. "Then we can pull you up."

"Tie it round me?" Charlie looked at the moat and the wall beyond. "And have you haul me through that water and up that wall? I tried drowning yesterday, if you remember. And it wasn't nice. And being hauled up that wall like a fish on the end of a line won't be any better. Can't you think of anything else?"

"It's either that or fly," said Kate grimly. "And you'd better make up your mind quickly: Hubert is waking up."

"Come on, Charlie. Be brave! You can do it!" Daniel encouraged her.

Charlie glanced over her shoulder. The gorilla had opened its eyes and was trying to struggle to its feet.

She hurriedly tied the rope round her middle. She stood up straight. "You're right, Daniel," she said bravely. "My mother always told me that

Charliopeaians are afraid of nothing." She shut her eyes tightly and sang in a quavery voice:

I'm a monster so terribly brave
Who looked for a maiden to save
I've just knocked out a monkey
As big as a donkey
When I climb up the wall won't you
waaaaaa...

The last word ended in a screech as Charlie was jerked off her feet and dragged into the moat. Kate gave the red-haired keeper a hand to pull her through the water and up the wall. It *was* like pulling in a fish, Daniel thought, as he watched the bedraggled furry bundle swinging at the end of the rope: only Charlie looked more like a baby walrus than a mackerel. But at least she was safe.

"Honest, Charlie. How could you?" Daniel asked, once Mr and Mrs Wilson had driven them home in disgrace and sent them up to their rooms. "You promised me you'd stay hidden and behave yourself."

"It was greed," said Kate. "Pure greed. She just wanted a piece of chocolate cake."

"I like cake," Charlie sniffed. "And nobody ever leaves me a piece. At home, when Mummy cuts the spludpuddery cake, I'm always left till last and I only ever get a tiny slice. Sometimes I don't get any at all. I thought it would be different here on Earth. I thought, when that monkey knew I was a visitor from another planet, he'd be willing to share. We're very particular about hospitality on Charliopeaia Minor, you know."

"I don't call stealing someone's cake and then knocking them out very particular," Kate told her.

Charlie put the end of her tail in her mouth and turned her back on them.

"How did you knock him out, Charlie?" Daniel asked. "Was it the same way as you exploded Kate's football yesterday?"

"It was only a little zappit wave," Charlie whispered, still with her back to them. "Only a teensie-weensie one. I know I'm not supposed to use them, except in the direst emergency, and I'm sorry I hurt your friend Hubert. But he wasn't nice. He was going to eat me up."

Daniel thought excitedly of all the things he could do if he had the same power as Charlie. "Can anyone use…what did you call them? …zappit waves? Could you teach me how to?" he asked.

"Why?"

"I could…" Daniel thought quickly, "I could burst the light bulbs in class or blow up the vase of flowers Mrs Murray always has on her desk…Or, if someone annoys me in the playground, I could knock them out just like you knocked out Hubert. It'd be great fun."

Charlie took her tail out of her mouth and turned round. Her eyes were crossed, Daniel noticed, and her whiskers had started to hum. "That's not what they're for," she said.

"Please!" Daniel pleaded. "I mean, I wouldn't really hurt anyone. I promise."

Charlie looked sad. The humming noise from her whiskers hiccupped and stopped. "I loved reading my book about Earth," she said very,

very quietly.

"You mean the one about Saint Patrick the Dragon?" Kate couldn't help asking.

"It was all wrong, though," Charlie went on. "And not only..." her black eyes flashed suddenly, "...about Saint Patrick and dragons."

Kate blushed.

"It said," Charlie went on slowly, "it said that Earth was a nice friendly planet."

She sniffed away a tear.

"It isn't friendly and it isn't nice," she said, "and I want to go home."

9

In Which Charlie Goes Home

Charlie woke up the next morning still feeling sad. She missed Charliopeaia Minor and the thunkelberry trees and the frumpus bushes and grunch-and-whoppit sandwiches.

She even missed her mother.

So when Daniel threw back the duvet, spilling her off the bed, and then tripped over her on the way to the bathroom, it was the last straw. She dragged the duvet into a corner of the bedroom, pulled it up over her head and sulked.

When he came back to get dressed, he didn't even notice.

Charlie let out a loud sob.

Daniel jumped.

Charlie sobbed again. Once she had started, she found, she just couldn't stop.

"Is that you, Charlie?" Daniel asked. "Where are you?"

Charlie sobbed even louder.

Daniel noticed the heaving duvet in the corner. He pulled Charlie out of it and picked her up.

"It's all right, Charlie," he said gently. "Do you want to tell me what's the matter?"

Charlie buried her face in Daniel's school jumper. "I wish I'd never come to Earth," she moaned. "People try to drown me and shoot me with footballs and drag me through rivers and up walls and monkeys try to murder me...I want to go home!"

Daniel gave her a hug. "Nobody wants to hurt you, you idiot," he said. "It was all your own..." He stopped. "We love you," he said instead. "We want you to stay here, you know that."

"You've a funny way of showing it, then," Charlie sniffed.

Daniel sighed. "Look, Charlie, I don't have time now. We'll talk about it when I get home from school."

Unfortunately Daniel's mother was late picking him up from school that day and insisted on stopping at the library on the way home. Daniel found himself getting more and more worried.

As soon as they reached the house, he rushed in, shouting for Charlie.

There was no reply.

He looked in the kitchen, the front room, even the dining room: no Charlie. He raced upstairs and looked in his own room, in Kate's and in his parents': they were all empty.

Slowly he came downstairs again.

"Charlie's gone," he said to his mother in the kitchen.

"Gone? Are you sure?"

"She was talking about going home this morning." Daniel found it difficult to speak. It was as if he'd swallowed a ball of spaghetti and it had jammed in his throat. "She said she hated Earth. I should never have gone to school and left her alone."

"Maybe she's just hiding somewhere," Mrs Wilson said. "Why don't you sit down and watch TV while I make us a cup of tea. She'll probably turn up when she hears me put the kettle on. For such a small monster, she certainly likes her food."

Daniel turned on the television. The picture was a fuzzy blur and the only sound to come from it was a high-pitched whistle.

His mother came in with a tray. "Oh dear," she said. "I'll have to get the man to it." She turned it off.

The whistle continued.

"That's Charlie!" Daniel jumped up. "Where is she?"

"I think it's coming from outside," said his mother.

Daniel ran out into the front garden. The whistling was louder now, but there was still no sign of Charlie.

He looked round: where was it coming from?

He looked up.

He had heard of people's blood running cold; now he knew what it meant. It was as if the Snow Queen had laid a finger on him and turned him to ice. For a minute he couldn't move, couldn't even shout...

The moment passed.

"Charlie!" he yelled. "Keep calm! I'll get help."

Charlie was up on the ridge of the roof. She was hanging upside down from the television aerial and screeching like a train trying to frighten a herd of cows from the line. If she heard Daniel, she didn't give any sign.

Mrs Wilson came to the door. "What's the matter, Daniel?"

"Call the fire brigade, Mum! Charlie's up on the roof. Hurry! Before she falls off!"

Mrs Wilson looked up. Charlie was still holding onto the television aerial with her webbed toes, but was now swinging round and round, as if she was practising for the gymnastics competition in the Olympic Games. Her screeching was, if anything, getting louder.

"The fire brigade's got better things to do with itself," Mrs Wilson told Daniel. "Come down out of there!" she shouted to Charlie. "And stop causing all this fuss. You'll have all the neighbours round."

Charlie continued to screech.

Daniel looked across the street. Curtains were

twitching, Mrs Fitzgerald was already hurrying across the road, even Mr Smith from next door had come out to see what was going on.

"You'll have to call the fire brigade, Mum. She's too scared to fly down."

"If she got up, she can get down, Daniel. Don't you worry about her. Just try to get her to stop making such a racket, or we'll have the police round for causing a nuisance. I'm going back in: I've had a hard morning at work and I need a cup of tea." Mrs Wilson went back inside the house.

"Come down, Charlie," Daniel shouted. "Just flap your wings and you'll fly."

Charlie stopped swinging for a moment. "I want to go home!" she shouted back. Then she whirled round faster and faster while her whiskers resumed their incredible screeching noise, sounding just like a jammed siren in a police car.

Suddenly she stopped and listened.

Daniel listened too. He could hear nothing.

Charlie swung round the aerial again, screeching louder than ever.

Again she stopped and listened.

Again, Daniel listened too and couldn't hear a thing.

And then the screeching got even worse.

It grew until it sounded like the wind howling round the house in winter, like a banshee searching for the dead, like...like a mother calling for her lost child.

"Hey-you-what's-its-name!" it wailed. "Where ...are...you?"

Charlie's answering screeches grew more urgent.

A shadow fell over the house.

Daniel looked up. He felt his heart thudding in his chest. He had never been so excited in his life.

It was fantastic! A spaceship was hovering over his house! A real, live spaceship! It was round and fat and brown, with small circular windows like portholes round the edge. It looked, in fact, exactly like a crumpet. Its engine was making a low whirring noise, but this was almost completely drowned out by the whistling coming from inside it.

Daniel's mother came running out of the front door again.

"Oh no you don't!" she shouted up at it. "I'm not having a spaceship in my front garden! It'll ruin the grass—and I've only just got the roses to flower. Go away! Shoo!"

Nobody paid any attention to her. The noise from the spaceship grew worse, Charlie's screeching was still loud but it was happier somehow, and the spaceship gradually sank lower and lower until it was level with the ridge of the roof.

One of the portholes opened. A ramp came down and stretched out towards Charlie.

"Don't go, Charlie!" Daniel shouted. "I want you to stay! You're my friend!"

Charlie stopped screeching. She looked down. She looked towards the spaceship. She started to whistle again, but sort of conversationally, not in panic.

Then she looked down at Daniel again, took a deep breath, shut her eyes tightly, flapped her wings and...jumped.

Daniel watched the little monster flutter down towards him. He caught her in his arms. "Charlie! I thought I'd lost you! I'm so glad you've come back."

Charlie gently squeezed out of his embrace and clambered down to the ground. "I'm sorry, Daniel," she said. "I liked having you as a friend. But I have to go home now."

She turned to Mrs Wilson. "Thank you very much for having me," she said politely, holding out a green claw to be shaken. "My mother hopes that you will come to Charliopeaia Minor and visit us some day. You are very welcome, she says."

Mrs Wilson put her arms round the little monster and hugged her, just as she hugged Daniel himself when he'd been very good. "Goodbye, Charlie. Tell your Mummy I think you're a lovely monster. Good luck!"

"You do?" Charlie beamed, her blue eyelashes fluttering in pleasure. She turned to Daniel and sang:

I've loved meeting you
And you've loved meeting me.
For I'm a lovely monster
As lovely as can be.
(*Your mother said so!*)

But I'd love to go back home again
To lovely Charliopee
So I give my love to everyone
And I take your love with me.

"Do you have to go?" Daniel asked. "You've only just come."

"Yes," Charlie said simply. "Say goodbye to Kate for me."

She looked up at the spaceship. "I'm ready now," she shouted.

"Then fly up, you idiot!" came a voice from the spaceship.

Charlie's eyes started to mist over again.

Daniel wiped a fist across his own eyes. He made himself smile. "Go on, Charlie! You can do it! You're Charlie now, not just Hey-you-what's-its-name. Didn't you hear Mummy tell you how great you are? And you're brave too, remember? You knocked out a gorilla, didn't you? What's a little flying to someone as brilliant as you are?"

Charlie smiled a wavery smile. "I did, didn't I? And I am!"

She flapped her wings more strongly.

"Goodbye, Daniel. Don't forget me. Maybe I'll see you again, some time."

"I hope so," Daniel shouted as the tiny monster, like an oversized bit of thistledown, whirled up into the air towards the spaceship.

The hatch closed behind it, the spaceship's engines whirred, Daniel and his Mum (and, of course, Mrs Fitzgerald and Mr Smith) were almost knocked off their feet by a gust of wind which flattened the grass on the lawn and blew the petals from the last of Mrs Wilson's roses.

And then the spaceship soared up into the sky, becoming smaller and smaller until it was just a tiny dot and then nothing at all.

"Do you think she'll be all right?" Daniel asked.

Mrs Wilson put her arm round him. "I'm sure she will. Her mummy may sound a bit impatient, but she obviously loves her. She wouldn't have come all this way back for her otherwise, would she?"

"I suppose not."

Daniel hoped his mother was right.